Phil of the Future™

Blast from the Past

Adapted by N.B. Grace

Based on the television series, "Phil of the Future", created by Douglas Tuber & Tim Maile

Part One is based on the episode written by Dan Fybel & Rich Rinaldi

Part Two is based on the episode written by Danny Kallis

Watch it on
Disney CHANNEL® · abc Kids™

Disney PRESS

VOLO

New York

D1292974

Printed in the United States of America

First Edition
1 3 5 7 9 10 8 6 4 2

Library of Congress Control Number on file.

ISBN 0-7868-3847-7

For more Disney Press fun, visit www.disneybooks.com
Visit DisneyChannel.com

PART ONE

CHAPTER ONE

It was a dark and peaceful night. A soft breeze blew through the trees. Moonlight glimmered on the lawn. Mr. and Mrs. Diffy were fast asleep in their comfortable bed on the second floor of their lovely home. Everything was just as it should be—until a loud crash of breaking glass sounded from downstairs.

Mr. Diffy shook his wife awake. "Honey, wake up!" he cried. "I think I heard something."

Mrs. Diffy awoke immediately and sat straight up in bed. "What was it?" she asked as she jumped up and pulled on her robe, ready to do battle.

"Go down and check it out," Mr. Diffy suggested. "I'll hang back and guard the bed." His wife looked at him in disbelief. She was supposed to face an intruder all by herself and he was going to "guard the bed"? Before she could protest, he added, "Can you bring me back a snack?"

"A snack?" Mrs. Diffy couldn't believe her ears. Burglars could be rampaging through their home, and her husband was thinking about having a bite to eat!

Mr. Diffy smiled at her. "Yeah, anything. Just surprise me."

In one swift movement, she snatched the comforter away and pulled her husband off the bed. "Surprise!" she yelled.

Her husband yelped in shock.

"You're coming with me," Mrs. Diffy said firmly.

Together, they crept downstairs to find that

their kids, Phil and Pim, were already there. They had also been awakened by the crash. Now the family looked around the kitchen, noting the signs that a mysterious intruder had been there.

Mrs. Diffy held up a pan which, until a short time ago, had been filled with her delicious lasagna, already cooked for tomorrow night's family dinner. Now, just a few scraps were left.

"Well, looks like *something* really enjoyed my lasagna," she said.

Pim held up an oven mitt with a huge bite taken out of it. "Don't flatter yourself, Mom," she said. "It also enjoyed your oven mitt."

"Maybe we have mice," Phil suggested. Mice wouldn't be so bad. Mice could be dealt with. Although, he thought, that bite looked awfully big for a mouse.

His mother nodded and turned to his father. "Honey, looks like we need an exterminator."

"Nonsense," Mr. Diffy said with confidence

as he took a plate of sandwiches from the refrigerator. "I can handle whatever's crawling around this house. Tomorrow morning, I'll go down to the hardware store and get some of that sticky paper."

Mr. Diffy's eyes gleamed as he looked at the two sandwiches, piled high with sliced turkey, cheese, lettuce, and tomatoes—not to mention that special gourmet mayo! Yum. "But right now, I want to slam down one of these bad boys for a little late-night pick-me-up."

Behind them, unseen by anyone in the Diffy family, the cupboard door under the sink slowly opened, revealing a caveman crouching under the pipes. His hair was long and matted, and he wore a tunic and boots made of fur. A leather cord strung with several large pointed teeth hung around his neck.

Unaware that their nighttime visitor was still in the room, Phil eyed the other sandwich. "Leave the other one out, too, Dad," he said. "I could go for a little nosh myself."

"Good call, son." Mr. Diffy laughed. "The po'boy sandwich was one of this century's great discoveries."

Sniff, sniff. The caveman could smell the sandwiches from across the room. And he had to agree with Mr. Diffy and Phil—they smelled absolutely *delicious*. He crept out of the cupboard and began cautiously moving across the kitchen.

Pim somehow sensed that something was . . . different. She quickly turned to look over her shoulder, but the caveman ducked behind the kitchen island even more quickly. Hmm, Pim thought, as she looked around the room, which looked completely normal. My nerves must be on edge with all this late-night excitement.

She turned back to see her father unwrapping the sandwiches with anticipation. Somehow, being awakened in the middle of the night and discovering signs of a mysterious intruder made a person very, very hungry. No one noticed the caveman as he sneaked out of the kitchen.

"Now, that's what I call a midnight snack," Mr. Diffy said.

Pim's and Phil's eyes lit up.

"Yeah, sure is," Phil said.

"Thanks, Dad," Pim said.

They each grabbed a sandwich and dashed out of the kitchen to enjoy their snack in their rooms.

"Oh . . ." Mrs. Diffy sighed as she and her husband watched the po'boys vanishing along with their kids.

A few minutes later, sleepy and still a little hungry, Mr. and Mrs. Diffy got back into bed, ready for what was left of a good night's sleep.

Mrs. Diffy made a face as she smelled something terrible. She looked accusingly at her husband. "Uh . . . Lloyd! Awww . . ."

"I didn't do nothin'," he protested. He wrinkled his nose. He hadn't done anything, but *something* smelled pretty rank.

Then he felt something warm push against his feet, and he laughed. "Honey, I'll take a rain check on the footsies, okay?"

His wife looked at him with horror. "That's not my foot. . . ." she said slowly.

She sat up, and they stared at each other. If it wasn't his wife's foot, Mr. Diffy thought, then what . . . ?

With one motion, Mr. and Mrs. Diffy flipped back the comforter—and revealed the caveman hiding at the foot of their bed!

Mr. and Mrs. Diffy screamed in shock.

The caveman screamed even louder in surprise.

Then they all screamed together, and the caveman jumped off the bed and ran out the door.

CHAPTER TWO

The next morning, the Diffy family gathered again in the kitchen, where they had found the caveman hiding once again under the sink.

Mrs. Diffy offered him a snack to lure him out. "Caveman wanna cracker?" she asked in a coaxing voice.

"Mom, he's not a canary," Pim said, rolling her eyes.

Mr. Diffy squinted at the caveman. "You know, there's something familiar-looking about this guy."

Phil nodded. "Yeah, I know what you mean."

He looked at their guest more closely. "Wait a second!"

The caveman grunted as if he were responding to Phil's excitement.

Phil continued. "Isn't he that goofy guy we met on our trip to the prehistoric times?"

They all remembered that trip. One of the highlights had been Phil and Mr. Diffy's rescue of a caveman from a deep hole; they'd had to pull him out with a rope, and the caveman had seemed to be very grateful.

"I'll never forget how he smelled," Mr. Diffy said. "Never would have seen him if I hadn't dropped my keys in there."

Now he looked more closely at the caveman in their kitchen and saw the resemblance to the caveman they had saved. "You're right," he said to Phil. "He must have stowed away in our time machine."

Well, that was one mystery solved, Phil thought. Of course, there was still the problem of what they were going to do with a stowaway caveman. Just as he was turning his attention to that issue, he heard a knock, and then Keely walked through the kitchen door. "Hey! You almost ready for school?" she asked brightly. At the sight of the Diffy family crouched around the kitchen sink, she looked puzzled.

The caveman grunted at hearing a new voice. "What's going on?" Keely asked as she knelt down to look into the cupboard that seemed to fascinate Phil's family.

Her expression turned from curiosity to shock at seeing a fur-wearing caveman crouching among the cleaning solutions and paper towels.

Pim hurried to explain. "A caveman stowed away in our time machine," she said. "He's now hiding under our sink, and I haven't had any breakfast." She sighed and rolled her eyes. "Welcome to my world," she added sarcastically.

Keely's shock was giving way to excitement. "Omigosh. This is unbelievable!" she exclaimed.

But the full impact of their situation was finally beginning to dawn on Mr. Diffy. "This is a disaster," he said, a little hysterically. "We've got to get him out of the kitchen. We've got to get him out of this house. If people catch us with a caveman, we'll be found out. Found out!"

Visions of what would happen if people realized that the Diffys were actually visitors from the twenty-second century began to flood his mind. The police, the government agents, the tabloid reporters—Mr. Diffy began to hyperventilate.

"Lloyd, breathe," his wife said firmly.

The caveman was starting to look a little scared, too. Phil leaned down to see if he could talk him out of the cupboard. "Hey, it's okay," he said reassuringly. "There's no reason to be scared. We won't hurt you." Phil took the caveman's hand and pulled gently, still talking. "C'mon out. It's okay."

The caveman grunted—a grunt that seemed

to say, "Okay, I'll trust you"—and slowly emerged from under the sink.

Keely looked on in admiration. "Wow, Phil," she said. "I didn't know you were so good with . . . cavemen."

Phil scratched the caveman behind the ears. "He's a friendly caveman," he said. He started talking to the caveman as if he were a dog. "Aren't you, big guy? Yes, you are." The caveman's left foot tapped the floor in delight. Keely started patting him and scratching his head, too, and the caveman's foot tapped even faster as he grinned contentedly.

"Phil, stop that before he goes on the floor," Pim snapped.

Suddenly, the caveman raised his head and began sniffing the air. He went to Keely's book bag and started smelling it.

"Oh, hey, I guess he likes peanut butter," she said.

He grunted in agreement.

She reached into the bag, pulled out a

peanut butter sandwich, and handed it to the caveman. "Take it," she urged.

Eagerly, he grabbed the sandwich and ran away, as if afraid that someone would take it from him. Phil thought the caveman might have the right idea, remembering how he and Pim had grabbed the po'boys the night before.

Before anyone could react, the caveman jumped over the kitchen counter and ran into the living room. Everyone yelled as he jumped on the couch, bounced a few times, then climbed on top of the armoire, still holding his peanut-butter-sandwich prize. He hissed and grunted a warning: no one had better try to grab *this* sandwich!

Keely and the Diffys stood back from the armoire, letting the caveman have his space, even as they wondered what to do next.

"I wonder what his name is," Keely said.

"I don't know," Phil said. "He looks kind of like a Curtis."

"Phil, don't you dare name him," his father

warned. "That's how it all starts." He gave his kids a hard look. He knew what they were thinking, and they could forget about it! "Look, we can't keep him," he said as firmly as he could. In these cases, he knew the most important thing was to hold the line.

Curtis sniffed the silk flower arrangement, then took an experimental bite. Hmm, not bad . . . but peanut butter was much better. He happily took another bite of his sandwich and grunted with contentment.

Mrs. Diffy shook her head. How, she wondered, had she ended up with a caveman crouched on top of her living room armoire, nibbling on her silk flowers, and eating a peanut butter sandwich? Did other mothers have days that started like this?

"This is not good," she said.

"If you need any help with Curtis, I'd be happy to pitch in," Keely offered, smiling up at the caveman.

"Stop with the 'Curtis' already. He's not

Curtis!" Mr. Diffy yelled. Then he turned to the caveman, who seemed to be making himself at home. "You're not Curtis!" he cried.

Curtis hissed at him.

"C'mon, Dad. I'll take care of him," Phil promised.

Mr. Diffy knew all about kids and their promises to take care of their pets. Hold the line, he told himself. Be strong. Hold. The. Line.

"Please, can we keep him?" Phil continued.

Pim watched the caveman, who was now smiling. She had to admit, he had a certain way about him, a certain charm. "You know, I've never used the word cuddly before . . ." she began.

Curtis let out an enormous, humongous, ear-shattering burp.

"Never mind," she said quickly.

Phil knew he had his father where he wanted him. Now, if he could just push him over the edge. . . . "Well, Dad?" he asked, looking as eager and hopeful as he could.

Lloyd Diffy hesitated. It was so hard to refuse his kids, especially when they had that eager, hopeful look on their faces.

"Let me think about it," he finally said.

"Yes!" Phil, Pim, and Keely all jumped in the air with joy. They knew what "let me think about it" meant. It meant, "Yes, you can keep him!"

"I didn't say yes!" Mr. Diffy protested.

"He said it again!" Phil exclaimed.

As they kept celebrating, Mr. Diffy sighed. So much for holding the line.

"**P**im Diffy, you are cordially invited this Friday for my Super Sleepover Extravaganza!" Debbie Berwick was walking down the school hallway at Pim's side. She was wearing a white shirt, pink sweater, and pink plaid skirt, an outfit that fairly screamed "perky to the max!" She was holding a clipboard with her sleepover invitation list and enthusiastically checking off names as she went.

Pim, who was wearing her favorite T-shirt, with the words BLAME MY PARENTS across the front, rolled her eyes and walked a little faster.

Unfortunately, Debbie had no problem keeping up. "Pim, you must not have heard what I said," she said.

Pim rolled her eyes again. She knew only too well how persistent Debbie was, and that she refused to take no for an answer. Pim stopped and turned to make her "no" so clear that even Debbie Berwick would get it.

"Here are some things I would never do: eat nails, stick my head in a toilet, or ride a man-eating shark," she said. "But I would do any of those things before I would sleep over at your house."

But Debbie wasn't listening. She was frowning at the list on her clipboard.

"Fudge-crackers!" she cried. "Pim, my grandma set the cap at twenty-five girls, and I've already invited that many. What a pickle . . . *maybe* I can squeeze you in."

I don't even want to go to this party! Pim thought. I don't even like Debbie! But the thought of barely making the invitation list is an insult!

"'Squeeze me in?'" she repeated. "Pim Diffy does not get 'squeezed' into anything." She grabbed the clipboard and glared at the names. She pointed to one. "Cynthia Chow . . . doesn't 'Chow' mean 'so long' in Italian?" she asked in a threatening voice. "Well . . . *ciao*, Chow."

Pim crossed Cynthia's name off the list and handed the clipboard back to Debbie. That would show her she couldn't put Pim Diffy on any wait list!

The next day, Phil and caveman Curtis were sitting at the picnic table in the Diffys' backyard, drinking lemonade. It was a beautiful, warm afternoon, and Phil couldn't have been happier. Curtis looked pretty contented, too. He had really settled in at the Diffys', even though he was at least thirty thousand years from home.

"It's been good having you around this past week, Curtis," Phil said. "I always wanted a little brother. Someone to show the ropes to, pal around with, you know?"

Curtis grunted as he stuck the straw from his lemonade up his nose.

Phil raised his eyebrows. He hadn't ever considered that showing someone the ropes meant telling him not to do *that*! Oh, well. "We still have some work to do," Phil concluded.

But even if Curtis still stuck straws up his nose, he had come a long way in just a week. In fact, Keely had spent a lot of time hanging out with them and taking pictures, so Phil could scroll through the digital files and see Curtis's progress.

Click! There was the time when Phil was teaching Curtis how to go out for a pass. He threw the football—a perfect spiral—but Curtis didn't get his hands up and *boink!* The football hit Curtis on the head.

Click! There was the time that Phil and Curtis traded clothes, just for a laugh. Phil looked like a complete doofus wearing Curtis's fur tunic, but he had to admit that Curtis looked pretty dapper in Phil's polo shirt and jeans. Of course, the flash on Keely's camera made spots float in front of Curtis's eyes, and he kept trying to catch the "fireflies"—but that was a normal reaction for someone who had never seen a camera before, Phil thought.

Click! Phil tried to show Curtis how to put on a pair of shorts—twice, in fact—but when Curtis tried he lost his balance and fell over. He just laughed at himself, though. One thing you had to say about Curtis the caveman—he may not have had many social skills, but he was really good-humored.

Click! Another try at throwing the football. Another football to the head for Curtis. This time, though, he picked the football up and threw it back—at Phil's head! Ouch!

Click! Then there was the time that Curtis came out of the house, holding the cordless phone and looking pleased and interested in his new toy. A little too interested, maybe.

"Curtis, no!" Phil had yelled, but it was too late. Curtis had eaten the phone. A few seconds later, Curtis heard a busy signal coming from his stomach. He rubbed his tummy, puzzled, then ran out of the backyard in a panic. Guess it *would* be pretty scary to hear a phone signal from inside your body, Phil had thought.

Click! One last try at throwing a pass—and this time Curtis caught the football! Keely recorded the wild celebration on her camera, as Curtis spiked the ball with a flourish, just like a pro football player, then danced around the backyard with Phil.

Phil smiled to himself. It was really fun having a caveman as a brother—even a caveman who ate the phone and couldn't put on shorts without falling over.

The next morning, though, Phil wasn't so sure. He and Keely were sitting in class, taking a test, when he heard a familiar voice grunt, "Ung-chagga!" in the hall.

He looked up and was horrified to see Curtis stalking past the door, holding his spear with two bags of cheese puffs stuck to the end.

"Scraps!" Phil cried, as he realized that Curtis was foraging for food.

Keely heard him and glanced up to see caveman Curtis. Quickly realizing the situation, she raised her hand and said, "Ahh, a robin is making a nest outside the window, Mrs. Friedlander. We'd all be missing an opportunity if we didn't look right this moment."

Her distraction worked like a charm. Mrs. Friedlander was known throughout the school for both her love of nature and her belief that no opportunity to learn more about the earth's flora and fauna should ever be passed up.

"Oh, really?" the teacher said with excitement, and she went over to the window to see for herself.

As she did so, Phil scooted out of the classroom and ran after the caveman.

"Curtis! Curtis!" he called.

Curtis laughed. "Ung-chagga!" he cried, pointing with pride to his cheese-puff booty.

Phil tried to reason with him. "Yes, good ung-chagga," he said. "Curtis, you've got to go home!"

At that moment, Mr. Hackett, a balding, nervous teacher, rounded the corner holding a newspaper. When he saw Curtis, he screamed.

Curtis followed his natural instincts. He screamed, too—then Mr. Hackett demonstrated courage that none of the students at H.G. Wells Junior/Senior High would have suspected he possessed. He glared at Curtis, then raised the newspaper he was holding and hit Curtis over the head.

Curtis growled. Mr. Hackett turned pale. Sometimes courage wasn't all it was cracked up to be, he thought.

Then Curtis lunged for Mr. Hackett's leg!

"No, Curtis!" Phil yelled.

Too late. Curtis chomped down on Mr. Hackett's leg.

Mr. Hackett, quite understandably, screamed again—louder this time.

Frantically, Phil pulled Curtis off the teacher, and they both ran as fast as they could down the hall and out of the school.

Left behind, Mr. Hackett dragged himself along the hallway toward the nurse's office, muttering, "Man down! Man down! Must get ointment . . ."

And that's how the legend of a man-beast that stalked the halls of H.G. Wells Junior/Senior High first began.

CHAPTER FOUR

"It's going to be so much fun," Debbie Berwick said happily as she led Pim down the hall toward her bedroom. Pim was carrying her overnight bag and had a trapped expression on her face. "We have fourteen pizzas," Debbie added.

How did this happen? Pim thought. How did she get from "I'll never sleep over at your house, even if you offer me a million dollars" to "Show me where to stow my stuff. I can't wait to spend the next twelve hours in your perky presence!"?

She shook her head. There was no use in

kicking herself for mistakes of the past. She was here now.

"What about soda?" she snapped at Debbie. "You got soda?"

"Nine liters!" Debbie beamed. "And some flavored soy milk. I hope you like staying up late 'cause we're going to"—she lifted her hands toward the ceiling—"raise the roof!"

Pim smiled weakly and repeated the raise-the-roof movement. After all, she thought, she might as well try to get into the sleepover spirit.

Debbie stopped in front of her bedroom door, barely able to contain her excitement. "Okay, ready to meet all the girls?" she asked.

"Let's do it," Pim said grimly.

Debbie flung open the door with a flourish.

"Hi, everybo—" Pim started. The words died in her throat. She gasped out loud as she saw the two girls waiting for them in Debbie's frilly, perfect bedroom.

"Silent Judy? Neck-brace Lana?" Pim cried out.

Judy, a scared-looking girl who never, ever spoke, stared at Pim through her wire-framed glasses. She didn't say a word in response. Big surprise, Pim thought.

Lana, an anxious-looking girl who wore a giant neck brace, protested Pim's description of her. "I get it off in eight to ten weeks!" she said proudly.

Pim grabbed Debbie and pulled her into the hall. It was time for a *serious* conversation, but at first all Pim could do was stutter, "Huh? What?" She pulled herself together and added, more coherently, "Please tell me your bathroom seats twenty-two."

Debbie pretended not to understand. "What do you mean?"

Pim gritted her teeth. "You said you invited twenty-five girls," she reminded Debbie.

"Nice turnout, huh?" Debbie said brightly.

What was with this girl? Pim wondered. Nothing seemed to get her down.

"Okay. Let's get this party started." Debbie

sounded even more cheerful than normal, if that was possible. "First, we're going to do a play I penned called *Magic Ballet Shoes*. Okay, let's go."

She waved a script in Pim's face. Pim groaned. This was going to be a *long* night.

Pim was right. An hour later, she was wearing an orange wig and a clown hat and saying one of the worst lines in modern theater to Silent Judy: "Are you finished building the canoe yet, Hobson?"

Silent Judy shook her head. She chopped away with her fake ax and said—surprise!—nothing.

Pim rolled her eyes and went on with her next line of dialogue. "Oh, dear. How will we ever get off this island?" she said.

Then Lana stepped in, delighted to have the spotlight for a moment. "Later that night . . ." she said dramatically. "Hark! I see a beautiful angel in the night sky."

Anytime an angel enters one of Debbie's plays, you can be sure who is playing that part, Pim griped to herself. Sure enough, Debbie seemed to float through the bedroom door, an illusion that was helped by the fact that she was standing on an old red wagon being pulled by Silent Judy.

Debbie wore a long white dress, sparkly angel wings, a halo, and an angelic expression. Her expression changed slightly as she caught sight of Pim; she even frowned a little as she saw Pim watching her with a sarcastic look in her eye.

"Bow to me, Pim," she commanded.

This is the final straw! Pim fumed to herself. "I quit!" she cried. "This doesn't make sense." She waved the script in frustration. "How does José go to work if we're stranded on an island? And the unicorn completely fell out of the story. And you said it was a comedy—where's the FUNNY?" She took a deep breath. Having finished her critique, she added more quietly, "I have to make a phone call."

Debbie looked confused and upset. "But . . . you'll miss your curtain call!"

As if I care about taking a curtain call in front of three dimwits like these, Pim thought as she stood in the hall, holding a phone to her ear and saying out loud, "Pick up, Mom. Bail me out of this nightmare."

She listened as the phone rang on, and on, and on. . . .

The phone was indeed ringing in the Diffy living room.

Unfortunately for Pim, the phone had been Curtis's afternoon snack. He looked at his stomach, confused by the ringing that he could hear from somewhere inside him.

Phil and his parents didn't notice. They were sitting on the couch, watching the TV news with focused intensity as the anchorman said, "We take you now to Yanoosh Ing, with a breaking story."

Curtis burped. Phones, he decided, were not the easiest things to digest.

On the screen, TV reporter Yanoosh Ing faced the camera, his face very serious. "I am live at H. G. Wells Junior/Senior High School, where a school administrator was reportedly attacked by a man-beast," he said dramatically.

On the screen, a small inset with Curtis's face appeared. Curtis touched Phil's shoulder, then pointed proudly at his picture. Phil nodded and brushed Curtis's hand away, nervously biting his nails. He had a bad feeling about what was coming.

The reporter looked into the camera and said, "I'm here with the victim, Neal Hackett."

The camera pulled back to show Mr. Hackett, pale and sweating, standing next to the reporter. Curtis grunted in surprise when he recognized Mr. Hackett on the TV screen.

The reporter turned to the teacher with a concerned expression on his face. "In your own words, Neal, tell America exactly what happened."

"Well, what can I say?" Mr. Hackett said

nervously. "I'm on my way to the powder room and, next thing I know, I'm being bitten on the leg by this giant freak show."

Phil and his parents exchanged worried glances as Curtis beamed proudly. The caveman wasn't sure exactly what it meant to be called a "giant freak show," but it sounded pretty good.

Mr. Hackett went on, trying to sound a little tougher. He already regretted using the phrase "powder room" while talking to all of America. "I was going to bust out with this judo throw that I learned, but I really need to be attacked from the side for that to work."

The reporter nodded seriously. "Are you offering any kind of reward for the capture of this man-beast?" he asked, hopefully. A reward always made the ratings go up.

Mr. Hackett looked at the reporter as if he were crazy. "On a teacher's salary?" he asked, incredulous. "Yeah, right, pal."

The reporter sighed. So much for winning the

sweeps season. He turned to the camera, squared his shoulders, and used his most theatrical voice as he said, "More on Beast Watch: Day One, at eleven."

The camera switched back to the anchor-man, and Mr. Diffy turned off the TV, upset. He turned to Curtis and asked, "How could you do this?"

Curtis looked confused.

"Dad, it wasn't his fault," Phil said. "Hackett hit him first."

"I don't care," Mr. Diffy replied. "That's that, all right? This Cur . . . this man-beast has got to go."

Phil couldn't believe it! His father was going to throw Curtis out, just like that? It wasn't fair! "Dad, you can't send him away," Phil said, trying to reason with his father. "He's . . . he's like family. Like a brother."

Curtis didn't seem aware of the danger he was in. He put his hand on Phil's head, pulled off a hair, looked at it quizzically, then ate it. He reached for another hair, but Phil brushed him aside. "No, Curtis, not now," Phil said.

"I'm sorry, Phil," Mr. Diffy said. "We're from the year 2121. We can't have the police snooping around here." He shivered. The more he thought about what could happen if people found out that they were time travelers from the future, the more determined he was to clean up this mess. Right now. He shook his head. "Nope. Loading up the car. Relocating him to Feek Meadows right this instant."

Mrs. Diffy reached out to pat Curtis's hand. "You understand, right, big fella?"

Curtis nodded, wanting to please her. Then he looked puzzled as he thought over what she had said, and ended up shaking his head.

No. He didn't understand at all.

CHAPTER FIVE

Feek Meadows was a beautiful place, Phil had to admit. He was walking through tall grass with Curtis, Keely, and his dad as they looked for the perfect spot to say good-bye to Curtis. Butterflies danced over the wildflowers, a soft breeze blew through the trees, birds chirped merrily. If you had to find a new home, Phil thought, you could do a lot worse than Feek Meadows.

Then, he shook his head. Nope, looking on the bright side just wasn't working. He had to make one last attempt to change his dad's mind. "C'mon, Dad," Phil said. "Curtis didn't mean to bite Mr. Hackett. You won't do it again, right, Curtis?"

Curtis was holding a flower that he had picked when they had arrived at the meadow. He smiled happily in response to Phil's question.

"Trust me, he'll be happier here," Mr. Diffy argued. "There's fresh air, room to roam, and there are probably other cavemen he can play with."

Phil and Keely looked at him in disbelief. Did he really think that other cavemen had managed to stow away on a time machine and zoom forward centuries into the future? "Could be," Mr. Diffy added defensively.

He stopped and looked around. "Okay. This is as good a spot as any right here. Let's say our good-byes."

Phil and Keely glanced at each other. This was going to be tough.

"Well, I guess this is it," Keely said. "It was nice knowing you." She tried to smile as she gave Curtis a farewell scratch behind his ear.

Then she held out a present. "I made you a good-bye bracelet out of rubber bands."

"Oooh . . ." Curtis said, his eyes widening.

Keely put the bracelet on him and pushed it up over his bicep. He smiled as he snapped it, pleased with the way it looked. Then he handed her the flower he had picked and gave her a hug.

Phil took a deep breath. Time for his good-bye speech, he thought. "Curtis, I'm really going to miss you," he said. "I'm sorry I didn't get to take you to a ball game like I said. But I got you this." He handed Curtis a football. "I thought you could remember me by it. You know, play with it."

Curtis laughed, remembering all the times they had practiced passing the football in the backyard—and all the times they had beaned each other on the head.

"Yeah," Phil said, smiling as the same happy memories ran through his mind.

"Okay, we're burning daylight, people," Mr. Diffy said, trying to wrap things up. "See ya,

Curtis." He pretended to suddenly see something far across the meadow, near a grove of trees. He pointed and said with excitement. "I think I spotted a zebra right over there. It was limping. There you go!"

Curtis stared intensely in the direction that Mr. Diffy was pointing to. He took a few steps, then looked back.

"Icha-tonga?" he asked Mr. Diffy, as if checking on the direction. Mr. Diffy nodded, and Curtis took off running in search of that night's dinner.

Phil and Keely sadly watched him go. It was hard to believe that they had become so close to Curtis in such a short time and that now they would never see him again.

Mr. Diffy clapped his hands. "Well, who's in the mood for ice cream besides me?" he said, hoping to change the mood.

No response. That's okay, he thought. The kids need some time to work through their emotions here.

"But first," he said, "I need to make a pit

stop. I think I saw an outhouse over yonder." He winked and added knowingly, "If you know what I mean."

"Yeah, Dad, we know what you mean." Phil sighed. "We always know what you mean."

As Keely and Phil watched Curtis disappear into the trees on the far side of the meadow, Phil couldn't help but wonder: what kind of life would Curtis have now?

"Now, I don't want to be a gossip, but a little birdie told me that in social studies, we're skipping chapter three and going straight to chapter four," Debbie Berwick said confidentially. Lana and Judy giggled with excitement; they couldn't believe they were trading inside information about social studies, straight from someone like Debbie Berwick!

"You always have the best dirt, Debbie!" Lana cried.

"Oh! I couldn't make it up if I tried!" Debbie laughed.

Pim rolled her eyes and groaned silently. The girls were now tucked into sleeping bags spread out on the floor of Debbie's bedroom. Pim felt as if she'd been trapped inside this stifling down-filled cocoon for days, forced to listen to inane chatter about who *really* deserved to be in honors English and who definitely did *not*.

She turned to Judy and said, "Judy, if I found a really big rock, would you hit me with it?"

Judy just stared blankly at her. Pim sighed.

Just then, the bedroom door opened, and Debbie's grandmother poked her head in. She wore a long, flowered dress with a cardigan, a pink kerchief on top of her gray hair, and thick glasses that magnified her eyes until they looked positively spooky. "Okay, lambies, it's six o'clock," Grandma Berwick said sweetly. "Lights out."

"Sorry, Nana, we lost track of time," Debbie replied, just as sweetly.

Pim couldn't believe it! What planet did these people come from? "Are you kidding?"

she said. "We can't go to bed now. It's still day-time. Birds are singing. People are swimming." She searched desperately for another way to make them see just how early it still was. "I can still burp my lunch!" she added.

"Don't worry," Debbie said. "We don't have to turn our voices off until six-thirty."

Yippee! Pim thought. Once again, Debbie had totally missed the point.

"And we still have to decide who's going to be crowned sleepover queen," Debbie added, clapping her hands in excitement.

Sleepover queen? Just when Pim thought this evening couldn't get any worse, it had.

Thinking quickly, she said, "I think I'm going to go brush my teeth." She grabbed her overnight bag. "Let me grab my toothbrush and the rest of my stuff."

Brilliant! Pim was congratulating herself as she crept down the hall. Maybe I'll become an escape artist when I grow up; I've definitely got the skills—

"Aaaggghh!" Pim screamed as she almost ran into Grandma Berwick, who was creeping down the hall in the other direction. She took a deep breath and tried for a quick recovery. "I was just going to the bathroom," she said weakly.

"Good, we can go together," Grandma Berwick beamed. "I need to spruce up my dentures."

Pim knew when she was outmaneuvered. "Nana Berwick, you don't cut a girl much slack," she said with reluctant admiration.

"That's why I'm still breathing, princess!" Grandma Berwick cackled. "Stow your gear."

Shoulders slumped in defeat, Pim went back into Debbie's bedroom and dropped her bag.

"Good night! Sweet dreams," Grandma Berwick cooed as she closed the door.

Pim stretched out in her sleeping bag and stared at the ceiling. You won round one, Nana, she thought. But Pim Diffy doesn't give up so easily.

CHAPTER SiX

"**D**aaaaad!" Phil yelled as loudly as he could, then stopped in the middle of the woods and listened as hard as he could. But he heard nothing except leaves rustling in the breeze and an occasional bird chirp.

He exchanged a worried look with Keely, who tried yelling, too. "Mr. Diiiiffffyyyyy!" she called.

Nothing.

"I don't understand," Phil said. "He should've been back by now. He was just making a pit stop. He didn't even have the sports page."

Keely tried to cheer him up. "I'm sure he'll be

fine," she said. "He seems like such an out-doorsman."

This was such a blatant lie that she couldn't deliver it with much conviction, but Phil appreciated the effort. Still, the longer they went without finding his dad, the more worried he became. . . .

. . . and if he could have seen his father at that moment, Phil would have been even more concerned. Mr. Diffy was stumbling through the woods, slipping on leaves and tripping over rocks. He had stepped off the trail for just a moment, to take care of that pit stop, but somehow he had gotten completely turned around. He had been wandering around for what felt like hours, and he had the nasty feeling that he was walking in circles. In fact, he was almost positive he had seen that big oak tree before. Maybe several times.

If only he could hear the kids' voices, he thought desperately. Then he'd know which way to go. If only they would yell his name. . . .

* * *

"Mr. Diffy!" Keely yelled.

"Dad!" Phil tried to shout even louder.

"Where are you?" Keely called.

"Dad!" Phil's voice was getting hoarse. He didn't know how much longer he could keep this up. If only his dad would yell for help, then they could follow the sound of his voice.

"Help! Help!" Mr. Diffy called out. He was getting really hot, so he had taken off his sweater and tied it around his waist. His face and hands were dirty from tripping and falling to the ground. And he felt that he was weakening every minute he continued to be lost in these scary woods. Whose idea was it to come to Feek Meadows, anyway? he thought indignantly. Whoever it was, they were to blame if he died out here! "Phil, Keely, help!"

Phil and Keely gasped when they saw Mr. Diffy's belt pack lying on the ground. "Oh. Oh, this is not good," Phil said. "My dad never takes off his belt pack. He takes a bath in his belt pack. This is all my fault."

Keely looked at Phil. How could he think this was his fault?

Phil saw her look and shrugged. "See, I wanted to keep Curtis, and because of me, my dad's missing."

Keely put her hand on Phil's shoulder. "Don't worry," she said. "We're going to find him."

Phil felt comforted by Keely's touch. Then another hand patted his other shoulder—but this hand was big. And hairy. And it was con-nected to an arm that belonged to—

"Curtis!" Keely said in delight.

Phil's face brightened. Even with his dad in trouble, he felt so happy to see his friend again. "You came back!"

Curtis nodded. "Ha-ta! Ng-guk atta-ta?" He seemed to know that they needed help, Phil thought. Maybe he was offering to pitch in.

"Ooooh, have him smell the belt pack," Phil

suggested to Keely. "Maybe he'll find my dad."

"Good idea!" Keely handed the belt pack to Curtis, who sniffed it deeply, then pointed into the distance.

"Un cha-cha!" he said confidently, and ran off in that direction.

Phil and Keely ran after him. After everything that had happened, Phil thought, it might turn out that Curtis was their only hope to save his dad.

This is my only hope to save myself from this sleepover, Pim told herself grimly as she settled the oversize glasses on her nose. As the other girls had nodded off, Pim had pulled together the perfect Grandma Berwick outfit: flowered dress, frumpy sweater, kerchief, and glasses.

Her plan was simple: sneak out of the house dressed as Grandma Berwick, then make a run for it. No one, certainly not Silent Judy or Neckbrace Lana, would dare to tackle the woman they now knew as Nana. Just to be on the safe side, Pim had waited until they were all sound asleep before putting her plan into action.

However, she hadn't planned on Debbie and her irritating ability to choose just the wrong moment to regain consciousness. Sleepily, she sat up and peered through groggy eyes at Pim standing before her in full grandma gear.

"Nana, what are you doing?" she murmured, rubbing her eyes.

"Just checking on my little angels," Pim said in a high, cracked voice.

Debbie was starting to drift off, but she still managed to smile and say, "Aw, Nana, I love you so much—"

"Shut your pie hole and go back to sleep!" Pim snapped. Sentimentality was all very well, but enough was enough. She had to get out of here.

Fortunately, this response must not have been too out of character for Grandma Berwick, because Debbie merely smiled and put her head back down on the pillow. Pim took a moment to watch her sleepover pals and to make sure that no one was close to being awake.

Satisfied that they were all still sleeping deeply, she said, "Sweet dreams, suckers," and crept out of the room and into the hallway . . .

. . . only to see Grandma Berwick coming toward her from the other end of the hall!

"Nana!" Pim said in a panic. She glanced around her. No escape route. No place to hide. No way out—unless . . .

Quickly, Pim dashed to an extra room that was being used for storage. It was crammed with old furniture and other odds and ends, but she had just enough room to stand in the door-way, absolutely still. Maybe if she didn't move a muscle, she thought, Grandma Berwick wouldn't even notice her. After all, her eyesight was terrible.

No such luck.

Grandma Berwick stopped dead in her tracks, mesmerized by what seemed to be her own reflection. "I don't remember a mirror being here," she said. She took a closer look. "Hmm," she said, straightening her kerchief.

Pim quickly mimicked her move, adjusting her own kerchief.

Grandma Berwick squinted, then bared her teeth. Pim did the same. Then—ooh, gross!— Grandma Berwick started *picking her teeth*! Keep calm, Pim thought. Don't look disgusted. Just pick your teeth exactly the same way Grandma Berwick is picking hers.

This has got to be the worst thing I've ever had to do, Pim thought, as she picked away. The absolute worst . . .

But, of course, Pim was wrong. Because the next thing Grandma Berwick did was push her butt out, pat it, and then say to her nauseated "reflection," "How do you like me now?"

Pim's mind was reeling. The images she had just seen were going to be seared into her brain forever. She might need therapy to get over them. In fact, she probably would need therapy, *intensive* therapy—

Nana raised her finger to her nose, as if she felt a little tickle.

Quickly, Pim mimicked the gesture.

Nana's face wrinkled as if she were about to sneeze.

Pim wrinkled her face as well, and something about pretending that she was about to sneeze must have made her want to sneeze because . . .

"Ah-choo!" Pim sneezed.

Automatically, Grandma Berwick responded, "Bless you." Then her eyes narrowed as she caught on to what was happening. "Wait a minute . . ." she said slowly.

She turned toward Debbie's bedroom and yelled, "We got a runner!"

The other girls tumbled out of the bedroom doorway and stood in the hall, blinking sleepily at the confusing sight of not one, but two, Grandma Berwicks.

"I'm not a runner," Pim said. The last thing she had ever wanted to do was have a sleepover with these girls, but she didn't want them to think they had caught her red-handed in an escape attempt. "Who are you going to believe? Me or Granny McWrinkles?"

For the first time in living memory, Silent Judy actually spoke. ". . . was trying . . . leave . . . sleepover?" she asked, total bewilderment written all over her face. Why, she seemed to say, would anyone ever want to do that?

Debbie, as usual, saved the day through her total cluelessness. "Pim, I know you weren't trying to leave the sleepover," she said brightly. "You were just starting a new game of costume tag! Pim, you are so much fun. All those in favor of Pim as sleepover queen, raise your hands!"

The girls and Grandma Berwick all grinned and raised their hands. Pim sighed. Nana may have won round two, but Pim wasn't down and out yet. She still had a few more tricks up her sleeve.

CHAPTER SEVEN

Phil, Curtis, and Keely wandered through another section of Feek Meadows, still trying to find Mr. Diffy. Keely spied a sock on a branch and held it up for Curtis's inspection.

"Oh . . ." Curtis said, looking concerned.

Then he pointed to a hedge of overgrown bushes. A hole had been made in the hedge—a man-shaped hole. In fact, the hole looked very much like the shape of Mr. Diffy, if he had pushed through the hedge with his arms raised above his head in a panic.

In fact, Mr. Diffy *had* pushed through the hedge in a panic. Now he was wandering aimlessly, with his sweater tied over his head like a turban to protect him from the sun. "The sun always rises in the east . . ." he babbled to himself. "The moss grows on the west side of the street. . . ."

A loud animal shriek interrupted his confused thoughts. Mr. Diffy turned to see what had made that unearthly noise and saw a large bush shaking violently.

"What was that? What was that?" he called, his voice shaking. "Identify yourself!"

Another loud shriek. Now Mr. Diffy was really scared. Fortunately, he thought, I have a plan. And it's a really good plan.

He decided to pretend that he wasn't alone. In fact, he thought it might be a good idea if he pretended that there were, oh, say, *three* other people with him, ready to do battle with enormous, shrieking beasts.

"Tex, did you hear that noise?" he said loudly, as if speaking to someone else. He changed the sound of his voice slightly and answered himself, "Yeah, he'll never take all *four* of us!"

It was a good plan, and it might have worked, except that Mr. Diffy then saw a hairy snout, two sharp tusks, and beady black eyes emerge from the bush. It was a wild boar!

"Mommy . . ." Mr. Diffy said weakly, just before he fainted.

At that very moment, Phil, Curtis, and Keely rushed onto the scene.

"Dad!" Phil cried.

Curtis pointed at the boar. "Sha-ta!" Curtis yelled.

The wild boar roared again. It seemed even angrier than when it had had only Mr. Diffy in its sights, if that was possible.

Keely's eyes widened. "I think that thing is going to eat your dad!" she said to Phil.

"Wat-sa . . ." Curtis said as he gestured for the boar to leave the area. Phil didn't know what "wat-sa" meant, but it sounded good. It sounded as if Curtis knew what to do. At least, Phil hoped so.

The boar roared again. Curtis roared right back at him.

This didn't seem to bother the boar. It roared again, even louder.

This time, Curtis didn't bother trading roars. Instead, he reared back and threw the football that Phil had given him—hard. It hit the boar right in the head! The boar screeched in pain.

"Huh!!!" Curtis shouted in triumph as he did a wild touchdown dance.

Phil and Keely ran to Mr. Diffy, who had recovered from his faint. As they helped him to stand, Phil asked urgently, "Dad! Dad, are you okay? Are you okay?"

Mr. Diffy shook his head to clear it. "Am I okay?" he asked. "Of course, I'm okay."

"Good job, Curtis," Keely said.

Curtis shrugged modestly.

"Curtis, you saved his life," Phil added.

Curtis smiled sheepishly and waved off the compliment.

The emotion was getting pretty thick around

here, Mr. Diffy thought. Probably best to nip it in the bud, before anyone starts crying. "Well, we should probably head back to the car," he said briskly. "Let's say our good-byes."

He started to stride off to the car, but Phil stopped him and pointed in the opposite direction. "Dad, the car's this way."

"Of course it is," Mr. Diffy said, recovering quickly. I couldn't have the kids think that I don't know where I'm going, he thought. They might panic. "That's the way I was going. I know where we are."

"I know, I know . . ." Phil said as he and Keely looked at each other and shook their heads.

As they traipsed after Mr. Diffy—now headed in the right direction—Phil said, "Curtis, the first time I saw you, I thought you were cute and cuddly."

Curtis smiled at the compliment.

"But you're not," Phil went on.

Curtis shook his head, confused. "Pets are cute and cuddly," Phil explained. "You're a person."

He stopped and looked Curtis in the eye. "I'll never forget you. Bye, Curtis."

Sadly, Curtis answered, "'Bye, Ph-il," and walked off.

Keely looked amazed. "Ohmigosh. What did he just say?"

"I think he just said his first words," Phil said, surprised.

They exchanged big smiles. Finally, Curtis had said two words in English—and one of them was Phil's name! Phil couldn't get over it.

Even Mr. Diffy seemed moved by the moment. "Curtis, wait," he called, then ran after him. Curtis stopped and looked quizzically at Mr. Diffy.

Mr. Diffy hesitated. After all, he had told the kids in no uncertain terms that they couldn't keep a caveman. And they would be risking a lot if they were discovered. And he had a clear obligation to protect his family.

But then, Curtis *had* saved his life. Mr. Diffy came to a decision. He cleared his throat and said, "The garage is cold and the roof leaks, but you're welcome to stay there. That is, if you promise to just lay low and not chase the neighbor's cat."

A huge smile broke out on Phil's face. "Curtis, you can stay," Phil said. Just in case the caveman didn't understand, he added, "That's good!"

"This is so great!" Keely cried.

Curtis was so happy, he laughed out loud. Phil turned to his father. "Thanks, Dad!"

Curtis laughed again.

Mr. Diffy couldn't help but smile to see how happy he had made everyone. "Let's head back to the car," he said, setting off in what he was sure was the right direction.

Phil coughed and said, "Dad, the car's that way."

Mr. Diffy looked in the direction Phil was pointing to. "That way?"

"Yeah." Phil nodded, trying not to make too big a deal out of it.

Mr. Diffy shook his head. "I made a wrong

. . . sorry." He didn't know if he'd ever get the hang of directions, he thought. But as long as he had Phil around, maybe he didn't need to!

As they walked across the field, Keely said eagerly, "So, Curtis, can you say 'Keely'?"

"Phil," Curtis said, proud of his accomplishment.

Keely frowned slightly and shook her head. "Uh . . . Kee-lee," she said, enunciating each syllable carefully.

"Phil," Curtis responded, grinning.

"Keely, don't confuse him," Phil said. "It's all right."

Curtis took off running, laughing, and saying his new word over and over. "Phil, Phil, Phil, Phil, Phil!" he chanted, then he stopped and threw the football at Phil.

Phil, laughing, caught it. "All right, okay!" he yelled.

It was going to be fun to have a brother, he thought. Especially one who knew his name.

* * *

Later that night, all was quiet and peaceful in front of the Berwicks' house.

Until . . . a patch of grass on the lawn moved, and Pim's head popped up above the surface like a prairie dog's, her face covered with dirt.

As she took a deep breath of fresh air, she cried, "Sweet freedom!" and triumphantly held up the spoon she had used to tunnel out of the house.

Suddenly, she heard loud barks and growls. They were definitely *not* nice barks and growls—and they were coming closer.

Her expression changed from happiness to fear as she saw the dogs running toward her, eager to catch an intruder. "Nice puppy!" she called out. "Nice Doberman! Go! Stay!"

Nothing she said was working! The growls were getting louder and closer and meaner. . . .

Pim popped back underground, defeated for the last time.

After all, she thought, there are worse fates than a bad sleepover. Above her, the dogs continued to growl. A *lot* worse.

PART TWO

CHAPTER ONE

The school day had just started, and already Phil Diffy was facing a challenge: getting a drink from the water fountain in the hall. He pressed the button, the water squirted up, he leaned down to drink, and the spout of water disappeared. Phil hated it when that happened!

As he tried again to get a drink, feeling like a complete dork, he heard a crash behind him. He turned to see a pretty blond girl standing at the foot of the stairs, her books scattered on the floor and a frustrated expression on her face.

"*Excuse* me!" she said in a Southern drawl to

the student who had just rudely pushed past her and made her drop her books. The other student kept on walking. The blond girl looked upset—but in a really cute way.

Phil forgot that he was thirsty. He walked over to the girl and said, "Oh, hey. Can I help you with that?"

The girl brightened instantly. "Why, *thank* you," she said. "These books are more slippery than a greased pig at a Fourth of July picnic."

Greased pig? Phil thought as he bent to pick up her books. At a picnic? What is she talking about?

He shrugged mentally and answered, "Yeah, I know what you mean."

The girl batted her eyelashes and smiled. "I'm Marla Beauregard," she said.

"I'm Phil Diffy," he replied, handing her the books. He looked more closely. She looked familiar. "Aren't you in Mr. Ginsberg's English class?" Phil asked.

Marla was delighted. He recognized her!

That meant he had noticed her. And in English class, of all places, where they studied poetry, the most romantic subject on earth!

"Well, I believe I am," she said flirtatiously. Now, if she could just keep him talking. . . . "Are you ready for that dreadful midterm he's cooked up for us?"

Phil smiled and shook his head ruefully. "No, I'm not." Mr. Ginsberg gave the hardest tests in the entire school. He always said that he believed that students should be challenged; Phil thought he just liked his reputation as the toughest teacher in the whole school.

The bell rang, interrupting their conversation. "Ah. We'd better get to class," Phil said.

Marla clutched her stack of books, which were already tilting to one side. She looked as if she was carrying every textbook she had, Phil thought. No wonder she ended up dropping some of them. "Here, let me take some of those for you," he suggested politely.

Marla looked astonished and delighted. "Oh,

my. You're going to help me carry my books?" she asked breathlessly.

What was the big deal? Phil wondered. She acted as if he had asked her to marry him, or something! Out loud, he said jokingly, "Well, if I carried *you*, people might stare."

Now she was looking at him with a really weird expression on her face. She was still smiling, of course—she never seemed to *stop* smiling—but now she looked kind of . . . *dreamy*. Maybe even a little starry-eyed.

"You coming?" he asked.

"Of course, Phillip," Marla said. "I'd follow you barefoot through a briar patch."

Barefoot through a briar patch? Phil thought. Where does she get these crazy sayings?

Oh, well. She seems nice, even if she does talk a little weirdly. He grabbed some of her books, and they headed off down the hall.

Pim Diffy sprawled on the living room couch, a bag of her favorite red licorice whips on her lap.

Her eyes were glued to the television screen, where a quiz show was playing at top volume. She watched intently, ready to take on any question the quiz show announcer could throw at her. She was pumped up. She was focused. She was in the zone.

"According to experts, a hundred years from now, kids will have no cavities," the quiz show announcer said. "True or false?"

"False," Pim said instantly. She took a big juicy bite of licorice. Ha! That was an easy one! Pim had so many cavities, she was on a first-name basis with her dentist. And since she and her family actually used to live one hundred years in the future—before they had taken their time machine out for a spin and ended up stuck in the present day—she figured she had a lock on getting *this* answer right.

"True," the quiz show contestant said. Pim smirked. This guy would never make it to the final round.

But before Pim could gloat over her easy

victory, the announcer said, "Correct! Okay, next question."

Correct? What kind of quiz show was this? The questions were ridiculously easy, and the answers were all wrong!

Annoyed, Pim talked back to the TV. "What, are you kidding me? I've got a mouth full of cavities!" She raised the remote control and pointed it at the screen. "And I've also got the clicker. See ya."

She changed the channel to her favorite cartoon, but before she could settle in, her dad, Lloyd Diffy, came up behind her, took the remote from her hand, and turned the TV off.

"Dad, what did I say about doing that?" Pim complained.

"Pim, you can't lie around the house every day," her father said firmly.

Pim rolled her eyes. Parents! They just didn't understand that television was educational, informative, and socially enlightening!

But her father had recently developed this strange notion that Pim wasn't well-rounded enough, just because she spent all her free time channel surfing. He went on to say the four words Pim had become used to hearing: "You need a hobby."

"I have one," Pim said quickly. "It's called 'television viewing.'" She was rather proud of her response: it was fast and funny and, most importantly, absolutely truthful.

As usual, her father didn't appreciate her wit. He shook his head. "I don't know what kids do in this century," he said. "I guess they play their 'sports' and they do their little 'music,' but you've got to do something. You're not going to waste your life lying on this couch."

He didn't want her to lie around on the couch? No problem! Pim immediately sat up and gave him a big smile.

"Or sitting on this couch," her father responded sternly.

Pim sighed. She knew when she had lost.

"All right," she said glumly. Then she headed out of the room in search of a hobby.

As soon as she had left, her father happily grabbed the remote, flopped on the couch, and turned the TV back on.

An announcer's voice came on. "For the extended forecast . . ."

Lloyd Diffy brightened. "Oh, the Weather Network," he said. Mr. Diffy loved weather, and not just local weather, either. He liked knowing what the weather was all over the world. Phil and Pim could never figure out why he was so fascinated with storms that were happening three thousand miles away, but they knew from talking to their friends that most parents had at least one strange quirk—and some parents had several.

Mr. Diffy settled back on the couch and began chewing on a licorice whip. "Oh, it's raining in Phoenix!" he said with interest as he watched storm-cloud patterns swirl over the Southwest.

CHAPTER TWO

The next day, Tia and Keely were sitting in the school cafeteria for lunch. Seth carefully ground pepper on Tia's salad from an enormous pepper mill that was almost half his height.

"That's perfect, Seth," Tia said. "Thank you."

But Seth didn't hear her. He was really concentrating. He needed to do a wonderful—no, fabulous—no, *spectacular* job of pepper-grinding for the girl that he loved.

Tia's eyes widened as she saw more and more pepper landing on her salad. "Whoa. Walk away," she commanded.

Seth didn't react. And he didn't stop.

"Uh, Earth to Seth," Tia finally said, loudly.

Startled, Seth came out of his pepper-grinding trance to see that Tia's salad was now covered with pepper. "Oh, sorry," he said weakly.

As Phil joined them at the table, Keely spoke up. "I'll take some pepper, Seth."

But he pushed the pepper mill over to her without taking his eyes off Tia. Keely sighed and rolled her eyes. In Seth's eyes, Tia was the only girl in the world, probably in the whole universe. Keely would just have to grind her own pepper.

Just as they all started eating their lunches, Marla walked up to the table with a big smile for Phil. She launched right into quoting a poem in her warm-molasses drawl. ". . . and even though the sun set, you've filled my heart with light," she recited with great feeling.

Phil paused for a moment to identify the poet. "Uh . . . David Butler Thurman?" he guessed.

Marla beamed. "Aren't you clever!" she said. Then she took a closer look at Phil's face and frowned a bit. "Oh, shug, you got a dangler," she said, pronouncing "shug" like the first syllable of "sugar." As a nickname, Keely thought, it was a bit too sweet, but then everything this girl said to Phil sounded positively syrupy.

Marla looked more closely at the spot of food. "I think it's puddin'." She licked her thumb and carefully wiped it off Phil's face, then smiled a big smile. "All better. See you after school."

As she flounced off, Tia and Keely looked at each other, then at Phil, their eyebrows raised in surprise.

"Uh, hello," Tia said sarcastically. "Yeah. What was that about?"

"What?" It took Phil a second to figure out what they were talking about. "Oh, Marla. Yeah. We're going to study together for Ginsberg's poetry test."

Tia and Keely exchanged another look, then Keely asked the obvious question. "Phil, do you like that girl?"

Phil laughed in disbelief. "*Like* her? No." He hesitated. Did Keely mean like like, as in, well, I-want-you-to-be-my-girlfriend like? No way! "You mean, *like*? No. I barely know her."

"Well, she likes you," Tia pronounced firmly.

Where do girls get these ideas, Phil wondered. "I don't think so," he said, just as firmly.

You would think that would end the matter, but then Seth had to wing in with his opinion. "Phil, I'm the last guy to get stuff," Seth said, stating the obvious. "But I think Tia's right." He giggled with glee. "That Marla likes you!"

Phil shook his head. This conversation had gone far enough. "Guys, she dropped one of her books, and I gave her a hand," he explained. "That's all."

Tia and Keely exchanged another meaningful glance. Each one knew exactly what the other girl was thinking: *Phil Diffy is clueless.*

Keely looked at Phil with a very serious expression as she decided to explain the rules of romance to him. "Phil, let me clue you in," she said. "When you do things for a girl, they have meanings."

Meanings? Phil started to feel confused and a little bit afraid. "Like what?"

"Like, if you carry her books that means you're interested," Keely said.

Tia nodded. "If you open the door for her . . ."

". . . that means you're interested, but currently seeing someone," Keely finished Tia's sentence.

"Giving somebody cuts in line . . ." Tia began, then Keely jumped in with the explanation. ". . . front cuts mean you think she's cute. Back cuts . . ."

Keely and Tia looked at each other again and spoke in unison. "Let's be friends."

Phil could feel his stomach turn over as he took in what they had said. He had given Marla the wrong idea—totally by accident!

And just because he wanted to be a good guy!

He glanced at Seth, hoping for support, and saw his friend busily writing on a piece of paper. Seth looked up and smiled. "Oh, don't worry," he said. "I'm jotting all this down for us."

"Great," Phil said glumly. He was in deep, deep trouble, and his buddy just wanted to take notes.

Pim walked down the school hall, her father's voice echoing in her head. "Pim," she could hear her father saying, "you can't lie around every day after school. You need a hobby."

A hobby! Where in the world could she find a hobby? Pim thought.

That's when she noticed the bulletin board in the hall, covered with signs advertising all kinds of school teams and clubs that students were urged to join. One particular sign caught her eye. The notice said that the school orchestra was looking for new members—and, most importantly, the orchestra rehearsal was happening right now. That had to be some sort of sign; after all, the sooner she got a hobby, the sooner she could talk her way back onto the TV-watching couch.

Pim ripped the paper down and headed for the auditorium. As she walked away, the bulletin board teetered, then crashed to the ground. But Pim didn't even notice. She was on a mission—a mission to make music!

As she walked into the auditorium, she heard the orchestra playing a beautiful melody. All the students seemed very serious and intent on the music. Especially the conductor, a short, blond kid wearing an oxford button-down shirt and a tie. He was waving his baton around with great concentration, a frown on his face.

After a moment, Pim realized that he would never notice her if she didn't do something, so she coughed. Loudly.

A pained expression crossed the conductor's face. Irritated, he gestured with his baton for the orchestra to stop, then turned to face her.

"We're not done yet, thank you," he said snootily. "You can sweep up later."

Pim scowled. Who did he think he was, talking to her like that? "I'm not the janitor," she snapped. "I'm here to join the orchestra."

He raised one eyebrow in disbelief. "Oh, really?" he sneered. "You have a name?"

Pim sneered right back. "Pim," she said. "You?"

"Bradley Benjamin Farmer," the boy said loftily.

Wow, three names, Pim thought sarcastically. I guess that makes you a triple threat in the land of the nerds. Then she caught herself. She wanted to join the orchestra, after all. It didn't make sense to get off on the wrong foot.

Time for some positive psychology. She smiled and said cheerfully, "So, what instrument do I play?"

Bradley laughed, a disdainful, mocking laugh. Then he stepped down off the podium—and Pim saw that he was more than a little short. He was a lot short. As in, he only came up to her shoulder!

But what Bradley lacked in height, he made up for in obnoxiousness. "Pim, I take my job very seriously," he said in a lecturing tone. "Meaning, I need musicians, not wannabes who waste my time."

Wannabes? Wasting his time? Pim gritted her teeth. She didn't even *want* a hobby, but she was being forced to find one, and now this little pipsqueak was trying to stand in her way? She didn't *think* so.

Pim took a step closer to Bradley and stared down at him. "Here's the poop," she said in the most intimidating voice she could muster. "I can't go home until I get a hobby."

Good. The pipsqueak looked scared.

Time to bring out the big guns. "In other words," Pim threatened, "find me an instrument, or I'm bunking at your house." Bradley gulped.

Very good. Now the pipsqueak looked terri-fied.

Minutes later, she was standing on the stage behind the orchestra and in front of a huge gong that was almost twice her height. She was holding a big mallet and watching Bradley carefully for her cue.

This is great! Pim thought. She had an instrument, she had a hobby, she got to hit a big gong—

Bradley pointed his baton at her. She swung the mallet and—*crash!* The entire gong fell over!

Bradley yelled in surprise and frustration. This girl couldn't even hit a gong!

But Pim grinned at Bradley and gave him a thumbs-up. After all, she was just starting out, and that wasn't too bad for her first try. She could only get better, right?

Bradley sighed and covered his face with his hands. What had he gotten himself into?

CHAPTER THREE

Phil and Marla sat in the library, their English textbooks spread open on the table. Phil had his head down, studying, so he didn't notice Marla as she gazed adoringly at him and fluttered her eyelashes.

Then she pulled an instant camera from her bag, pointed it at him and took a picture. *Flash!*

"What are you doing?" he asked.

Marla smiled. "Scrapbookin'," she explained.

Scrapbookin'? Phil thought, puzzled. What was she talking about?

She held up the instant photo. "This one's

gonna go right on the cover of my Phil Diffy edition."

He sighed. Marla seemed to have forgotten the reason they decided to get together after school. Maybe she just needed a gentle reminder. . . . "Marla, the poetry test is on Friday, okay?" he said. "So we really need to buckle down." Ah, here was a good opportunity to get things back on track! "You see, 'buckle down' is a metaphor for studying," he went on. "And a metaphor is . . ."

Marla eagerly finished his sentence. ". . . A comparison. But a 'simile' is a comparison using the words 'like' or 'as.'"

Great! Phil smiled. Now they were back to studying. Across the room, Miss Phipps, the librarian who was known for her grouchiness, was shelving books. Phil couldn't resist; he had to use her in a simile. "Miss Phipps is as crusty as a piece of toast."

Marla laughed loudly. Miss Phipps whirled around, frowning. "Shhh!" she hissed.

"And you are as funny as a mule in a bow tie," Marla whispered.

Uh-oh. Phil glanced over at a bust of a famous author sitting on the shelf. His imagination must be running wild—it looked as if the bust's head had transformed into Tia's head! She was frowning as she warned him, "Ah, ah, ah. Phil, whatever you do, don't try to make her laugh."

Startled, Phil looked away from the bust and quickly said to Marla, "I wasn't trying to make you laugh. I was just trying to give you an example of a simile. Are you on page twelve yet?"

"Almost," Marla replied cheerfully. She pulled out a pack of gum and offered it to him. "Want a piece?"

"Sure," Phil said, but as he reached for the gum, he saw the world globe at the next table start to spin until the oceans and continents were replaced by Keely's face. And now Keely was warning him, too!

"These are the rules, Phil," she said. "No

matter what you do, don't take anything from her. Gum, mints, nuts of any kind. Gum means one thing—commitment."

"Really?" Phil asked Keely.

Marla looked puzzled. "Really what?" she asked.

Startled, Phil realized that his question made no sense; he needed a quick save. Thinking quickly, he said, "I'm really not interested in nuts, mints, or gum of any kind."

Miss Phipps spun around again, frowning even more fiercely. "Shhh!" she hissed.

"All right," Marla shrugged. That Phil, she thought. He's such a sweetie pie.

The members of the school orchestra sat on the auditorium stage, listening attentively to Bradley as he gave them a pep talk about their upcoming concert.

"As you know, Friday is our big recital," he said. "Our performance will feature a talented young soloist who will sing a wonderful song."

Bo-o-ong! The gong sounded. Bradley looked to the back of the stage, irritated. Pim smiled.

"Pim! I said 'song,' not 'gong,'" Bradley snapped.

Bo-o-ong! Pim hit the gong again, then joked, "You gotta speak up. There's a lot of noise back here."

Bradley rolled his eyes and continued. "Anyhoo—without further ado, let me introduce our lovely soloist—" He made a grand flourish with his arms. "—Miss Deborah Berwick."

Ugh! Pim made a face. It figured that the star of the show would be Debbie Berwick, the most perfect girl in the school. The orchestra applauded as Debbie stepped onto the stage. She had a perfect smile on her face, her hair was cut in a perfect shiny bob, and her red headband perfectly matched the red bow on her dress. She looked perfect in every way.

"Bradley Benjamin Farmer, how are you?" Debbie said in a fake starlet voice as she exchanged air kisses with Bradley.

Ugh. Where do they think they are? Pim fumed. Hollywood?

"Debbie, you haven't aged a bit," Bradley gushed. "I haven't seen you in so long."

Double ugh. Time for Pim to step in—

Bo-o-ong!

At the sound of the gong, Bradley turned, frowning, and snapped at Pim, "I said 'long'!"

Debbie peered at the back of the stage. "Is that Pim Diffy on gong?" She sounded absolutely delighted to see Pim.

Pim couldn't help it; she giggled, pleased that Debbie had recognized her.

Bradley sighed. "Tell me you don't know her," he begged Debbie. "Please tell me you don't know her."

But Debbie prided herself on being relentlessly positive and upbeat. "Oh, of course I know Pim. She's a treasure. Hi!" She waved at Pim.

Pim couldn't help it; she waved back. Maybe Debbie Berwick wasn't so bad she thought. Maybe they could even be friends. . . .

Then, the rehearsal started. Debbie was going to sing "Give My Regards to Broadway." Pim's job was to hit the gong at the exact right moment.

Debbie launched enthusiastically into the song. She belted out the finale, "'Give my regards to old Broadway and say that I'll be there 'ere long—'" and Pim hit the gong.

Unfortunately, she hit it too early.

Debbie smiled forgivingly and started again. This time, she got to the finale, paused for the gong and—nothing. Everyone turned to look at Pim, who was daydreaming about lying on the couch and watching TV . . . oops. When she saw that everyone was looking at her, she quickly hit the gong and gave the orchestra a big smile to cover up her mistake.

Debbie didn't look quite so forgiving as, once again, she launched into her song. This time, Pim was determined to hit the gong as perfectly as Perfect Debbie Berwick would do it.

Debbie sang, "'And say that I'll be there 'ere long—'"

That was her cue! Pim swung and . . . lost her grip. The mallet flew out of her hand and landed offstage with a crash.

Pim winced. She didn't even want to know what the flying mallet had just broken.

She looked at Debbie and Bradley. "My bad," she said sheepishly.

Finally, the rehearsal was over. Pim knew she hadn't put on a stellar performance, but she was confident that she'd be all right on the big night. Maybe, she thought, it would be a good idea to reassure Debbie on that point. She had looked a little miffed after the tenth time that Pim had missed her cue.

As the rest of the orchestra drifted out of the auditorium, Pim walked up to Debbie and Bradley. "Hey, Debbie. I jumped a couple of those gongs, but don't worry," she said breezily. "I'll nail it tomorrow night at the concert. Who knew a hobby could be so much fun?" She turned to Bradley and waved a cocky good-bye. "Down the road, Farmer."

After Pim left, Debbie turned to Bradley. She didn't want to hurt Pim, but, after all, she was performing tomorrow night. In front of a huge crowd. Who would expect her, Debbie Berwick, to be Absolute Perfection. She really didn't have a choice.

"Um, to spare Pim some embarrassment, I think she should miss the concert tomorrow night," Debbie said. In case Bradley thought she was being mean, she added earnestly, "She'll thank us later."

Bradley smiled. It was really miraculous how he and his star performer were in perfect sync! "Brilliant!" he said happily.

Debbie nodded. "Good luck telling her!" she said briskly as she quickly left the auditorium.

Bradley stared after her, shock and dismay written all over his face. *He* had to tell Pim?

His doctor kept telling him that he was too young to develop an ulcer, but Bradley wasn't so sure. His stomach was really starting to hurt.

CHAPTER FOUR

The next day in the cafeteria, Seth was busily making a salad for Tia. And, since she was the girl he adored above all others, he tossed the lettuce with extra abandon, added a bit more vinaigrette than was strictly necessary, and threw in a few extra condiments for good measure.

Tia watched his movements carefully. "Hold the anchovies," she barked. "I hate those salty little devils."

Her every word was his command. Immediately, Seth flung the offending anchovy over his shoulder. He barely heard the scream as another student slipped on the small, slimy fish and fell on her face.

Then Phil joined them, and Keely and Tia turned their attention from salad-tossing to teasing.

"My stars, it's that heartthrob Phil Diffy," Keely squealed, imitating Marla's Southern drawl.

"Come here, shug," Tia said, in her own high-pitched version of Marla's voice. "You got a big ole dangler."

The girls giggled, but Phil didn't take offense. Their teasing didn't bother him, because they were way behind the times. "You know what?" he told them. "I think I've actually taken care of the Marla situation. I gave her nothing to misinterpret. In fact," he added confidently, "I think I've heard the last of ole Marla."

In just a few seconds, he would realize he had spoken too soon. In fact, the words were barely out of his mouth when a man dressed as an Olde English town crier—complete with a black velvet hat and red-and-gold tunic—marched into the cafeteria carrying a boom box and a trumpet. He put the boom box on the table, lifted the trumpet to his lips, and blew a fanfare.

Of course, every student in the cafeteria turned to stare at him. Once he knew that he had everyone's attention, he unrolled a scroll, cleared his throat, and bellowed, "Hear ye. Hear ye. Be it proclaimed throughout this land, H.G. Wells Junior/Senior High, that maiden Marla loves squire Phil."

Phil turned bright red as the room erupted into laughter. Nothing worse than this would ever happen to him again in his entire life, he thought.

But Phil was wrong. Something worse would happen in the next breath, because the town crier was not finished. He went on: "May their passion be borne on the wings of a thousand doves. This love decree hath ended."

Phil sank down in his seat and covered the side of his face with his hand, wishing desperately that he had the power to become invisible.

The town crier leaned over and muttered to Phil, "Yo, chief, you know where I can grab a cab?"

Phil stared at him. Didn't he realize that he had just ruined Phil's life? Apparently not. Well, Phil wasn't going to help him out. "Not a clue," Phil said. Let the guy with the trumpet find his own way home, he thought.

He turned back to his friends and managed a fake smile. "Hey! How about that?" Phil said cheerfully. "Marla must've met another guy named Phil."

His friends looked at him with pity. Nice try, Phil, their faces said.

Out loud, Keely said, "I don't think so, squire."

Phil glanced at the cafeteria entrance, where Marla and a gaggle of her friends were staring at him. Marla blew him a kiss, as her friends giggled. Phil groaned.

What had he gotten himself into?

Urgently, Keely said, "Phil, you have to do something. You have to talk to her."

Tia shook her head. "Forget talk," she snapped. "Kick her to the curb."

Phil felt his stomach do a flip-flop. "I have to break up with her?" he said. "How? I . . ."

He glanced around the table, searching for advice. But Keely shook her head. "Don't look at me," she said. "I've never broken up with anybody."

"Look, it's a snap," Tia said impatiently. "You know the guy I'm going out with, Mikey Watson?"

They all nodded. Seth got a faraway look in his eyes, as if he were imagining a terrible fate for Tia's boyfriend. "Mikey Watson, aka the luckiest guy in the ninth grade," he said grimly. "I've heard of him."

"I was going to cut him loose on Monday anyway, but if this helps . . ." She looked around the cafeteria and spotted Mikey sitting at a nearby table, talking with a friend. Tia called out to him, "Hey, Mikey!"

Mikey looked up and gave her a big smile.

There was nothing like having a beautiful girl like Tia call your name in front of everybody in the school, he thought. Now, everybody would know that he was dating one of the coolest girls at H.G. Wells Junior/Senior High. . . .

"These last few weeks have been huge," Tia said briskly. "But, we're done."

Mikey couldn't help it. He screamed in shock, then put his head on the table and began to sob. His friend put one hand on Mikey's shoulder to comfort him—but with the other hand, he made the "call me" gesture to Tia.

Tia turned back to her friends, satisfied that she had successfully demonstrated a fast and easy break-up technique. "See, painless," she said.

Mikey's sobs were still echoing around the cafeteria. Phil's stomach was doing more than flip-flops now; it felt like it was doing a triple-somersault dive off the high board.

"I can't do that," he said. Marla was a pain, but she was a nice person. He couldn't make her sob like that. Could he?

Maybe, Phil thought, it was time for a heart-to-heart talk with his dad. Mr. Diffy's experience with girls may have been far in the past—well, actually, it was far in the future, but whatever. He had to have some good advice for his son.

After school, Phil found his dad in the kitchen and explained his problem with Marla. "I don't know what to do," he said. "See, if I tell Marla I don't like her, it'll hurt her feelings."

Mr. Diffy beamed. This was just the kind of scene he had hoped to play out with his son someday. It was just like those classic father-son moments on those funny TV shows the kids watched all the time! "Son, it's a good thing you came to me," he said as he climbed on a step stool to get something from the cabinet. "This is what you call a classic father/son moment."

Phil felt relieved. "Really?" he said. "You mean, girls had crushes on you when you were growing up?"

Mr. Diffy hesitated, then admitted the truth. "No," he said.

Phil's face fell.

Mr. Diffy quickly added, "But they did on my old college roommate, Rex."

Hmm. Phil thought he remembered his parents talking about someone named Rex whom they both knew in college. . . . "Rex, Rex," he said, trying to recall what he had heard. "Isn't that the guy that Mom almost married?"

Mr. Diffy looked uncomfortable. "Let's not go there," he said quickly. He stepped down from the stool, blew the dust off a metal case he was holding, and took out a small device with a glowing dial. "Anyway, he had so many girls chasing him, he used one of these."

Phil took a closer look at the device. Incredible. His dad must have kept this since his college days! It belonged in a museum somewhere! "Oh," he said, "one of those old-fashioned DNA scramblers."

His father nodded. "Yup. I never go anywhere

without this thing," He chuckled, thinking of what the DNA scrambler could do. "Oh, they're a hoot at parties. It'll make you look so strange, Marla will be running for the hills."

This was his dad's solution? A party trick? Phil managed a weak smile and said, "Great. Thanks, Dad."

Mr. Diffy chuckled again as he thought of all the times he had used the DNA scrambler to get a laugh. "Hey, remember when I used it on your Uncle Milt and made his lips look like a fish?"

"Yeah," Phil said. "You really lightened up his funeral."

His dad laughed. "That's what I'm saying. Yep."

He walked out of the kitchen, still chuckling to himself. Phil sighed and stowed the device in his backpack. His dad's solution seemed like a long shot, but he didn't have any better ideas. He'd have to give the DNA scrambler a try and hope that Marla would freak out enough to leave him alone. Forever.

* * *

Phil decided to use the DNA scrambler the next time he and Marla were alone, which, fortunately, was the very next afternoon. They had agreed to meet in an empty classroom during a free period to study for their big test.

When Phil got to the room, Marla was already there. She gave him a huge welcoming smile, but Phil just said, "Hey, ready to study?" That was good, he thought. Laid-back, cool, making it very clear that they were just study partners, nothing more. . . .

"Ready isn't the word," Marla replied enthusiastically.

Oh, no, Phil thought. Her eyes were bright and sparkly, and she was smiling at him as if they were soul mates. He had the feeling that his attempt to steer them back to a "just friends and study partners" relationship was doomed to fail.

"So," Marla went on happily, "what did you think of my proclamation at lunch?"

As Phil reached into his backpack and turned on the DNA scrambler, he said, "Oh, that was a proclamation? I was wondering what that was."

"That was my uncle Jerry," she explained. "He does some regional dinner theater."

That blowhard in the fancy tunic was a serious actor? Phil searched his mind for some kind of tactful response. "Well, he is, uh . . . he is quite the thespian," he finally said.

He pressed a button on the DNA scrambler. *Bleep! Bloop! Blurp!*

The device did its job. Phil's head instantly grew to five times its size! He looked like the reflection in a carnival fun-house mirror.

Marla's eyes widened in shock. "Goodness gracious! Philip, there is something wrong with your head," she said nervously.

Play it cool, Phil reminded himself. "There is?" he asked innocently.

"Yes, it's really enormous," she said, her voice quivering.

Great, she's totally freaked out now, Phil thought. "Oh, goodness," he said, trying to sound casual. "Yeah, that happens sometimes. See, it's probably just a little reaction to all the chalk in here. Eh, what can you do?"

He pushed another button on the DNA scrambler. *Bleep! Bloop! Blurp!*

His head immediately went back to its normal size. Marla blinked. "Oh!" she said, looking concerned. "Phil, I think you should go to the nurse."

He shook his head. "No, I'm fine. Really. So, what do you say? Let's get started on those sonnets, huh?"

Marla eyed him nervously, but said, "Okay."

He hit the button on the DNA scrambler again. *Bleep! Bloop! Blurp!*

Now Phil's head shrunk to the size of a baseball!

"Aah!" Marla screamed.

Phil did his best to look innocent. "What?" he asked. "Oh, did my head shrink again?"

Marla nodded, her eyes even wider than before.

"Yeah," Phil sighed. "Well, I'll understand if you don't want to hang out with me anymore. Yup, I'm pretty grotesque," he said sadly. This is great! he thought. She must think I'm a freakazoid by now. There's no way she'll still have a crush on me. . . .

But something was wrong. Marla was smiling at him. She looked noble, gracious, even . . . saintly. "Now, Philip, I wasn't raised to judge a person on how they look on the outside," she said.

Oh, no. Phil's heart sank as he pressed the button for the last time. *Bleep! Bloop! Blurp!* His head went back to normal.

Marla continued, "What I care about, is what's on the inside. And, Philip Diffy, your insides are cuter than a bug's butt!"

Phil tried to laugh, but he didn't sound very convincing.

Okay, he thought. Time for Plan B.

Later that day, Bradley, dressed in a tuxedo with a red rose in the lapel, paced nervously backstage. The concert was scheduled to start in half an hour, but that wasn't why he was nervous. He always had total confidence in his own abilities as a conductor; in fact, he looked forward to stepping onto the stage in front of hundreds of people and giving them the thrill of a lifetime.

No, his anxiety could be summed up in two words: Pim Diffy. He had to give her the bad news that she wasn't going to play in the concert tonight. And, from his brief acquaintance with her, he didn't think she would take the news well.

He saw her walking toward him, and his heart lurched. Summoning all his courage, he said, "Pim, can I speak to you?"

Before he could launch into his speech—which he had rehearsed three dozen times in the last hour—she said excitedly, "Don't worry, I practiced my gongs all night. My dad said I sounded great—right before he left to get a motel room."

Bradley gulped. Direct and to the point, he thought. That's the only way to break bad news.

"Pim, there's no easy way to say this," he started. "I rewrote the piece, and we won't be needing your help tonight."

There. That was clear, concise, matter-of-fact. She couldn't get mad at him . . . could she?

He eyed her carefully and felt a surge of hope. Actually, Pim *didn't* look mad. She just looked confused. "You took out my gongs?" she asked.

Bradley nodded. "Yes."

Pim's eyes narrowed. Uh-oh, Bradley thought, his brief moment of hope dying away. *Now* she looks mad.

"Did Debbie Berwick put you up to this?" she demanded.

"No," Bradley said, his voice quivering just a bit.

Pim leaned in closer. It helps that I'm so much taller than this little pipsqueak, she thought. It made intimidating him that much easier. "Bradley Benjamin Farmer, look me in the eye," she said slowly, with as much menace as she could muster. "Was this Berwick's idea?"

Bradley wanted to hold out, but he couldn't. Pim was just too scary. After only three seconds, he folded. "She . . . she may have . . . suggested it," he said faintly.

Pim eased off a bit and smiled at Bradley. "Well, hey, these things happen," she said in an understanding tone.

Relief flooded through Bradley. Maybe

everything would be all right, after all, he thought.

Then Pim gestured toward the custodian's closet. "Can I see you in this dark, dusty closet for a quick sec?" she asked sweetly.

Oh, he thought. Everything wasn't going to be all right. "But, why?" he asked anxiously.

As an answer, Pim grabbed him by his carefully ironed tuxedo shirt and pulled him into the closet. Minutes later, she stepped out, alone, dressed nattily in a tuxedo with a red rose in the lapel.

"So you think you can ruin my new hobby?" she muttered to herself. "Think again, Berwick. Because there's a new conductor in town, and she's *nasty*."

An orchestra member who was walking by gave her a funny look. Pim pointed her baton at him and said fiercely, "You. Leave."

A girl dressed in a tux, talking to herself, and threatening him with a baton?

He ran.

Pim gazed at the baton that gave her so much power, and smiled with satisfaction. Tonight, she thought, is going to be *fun*.

A short time later, Debbie Berwick walked onto the stage. She was dressed in a beautiful, coral, floor-length dress that shimmered in the stage lights. The audience burst into applause, and she bowed graciously.

"Thank you, thank you," she said. "You're too kind. Thank you."

But she had only a moment to enjoy the spotlight, because just then Pim walked on-stage and began taking her own bows as the audience applauded.

Surprised, Debbie said, "Pim, what are you doing here?"

Pim smiled sweetly. "Bradley had an emergency," she explained smoothly. "He ran out of hair gel. Asked me to fill in."

Before Debbie could ask any more questions, Pim turned to face the audience. "Good evening, ladies and gentlemen," she said. "This first piece I will conduct—" She hesitated for just a second as she searched her memory for something, anything, to say about the song. Finally, she finished, "—was written a long time ago by a dead guy."

Debbie looked at her in disbelief. *A long time ago by a dead guy?* Pim was making a mockery of a great musical event!

But Debbie Berwick lived by one motto and one motto only: the show must go on. Pim raised her baton to get the orchestra's attention, then brought it down with a flourish. The music started, and Debbie gamely launched into "Give My Regards to Broadway."

She belted out the words like a musical-theater superstar: "'Give my regards to Broadway! Remember me to Herald Square!'"

It was going well, she thought. Very well, in fact. Her voice had never sounded better. . . .

Then the music suddenly sped up. The orchestra was playing at least twice as fast as normal! She glanced at Pim, confused. Pim smiled with sweet malice as she waved her baton in rapid-fire tempo.

Fine, Debbie thought. She sped up, too, as she sang, "'Tell all the gang at Forty-Second Street that I will soon be there!'" In the audience, her parents exchanged confused looks.

Just when she had the hang of singing at supersonic speed, the music slo-oo-owed . . . wa-aay . . . do-own. Debbie took a deep breath and slowed her singing down to the pace of a funeral march: "'Whisper of how I'm yearning . . .'"

Back to superfast! She sang the words as quickly as she could: "'. . . to mingle with the old-time throng! Give my regards to old Broadway, and say that I'll be there 'ere, I'll be there 'ere, I'll be there 'ere loooooo . . .'"

She held the last note, waiting for Pim to bring down her baton and end the song.

But Pim just kept her hands in the air, stretching out that last note. . . .

CHAPTER SIX

Meanwhile, across town, Phil knocked on the back door of the Teslow's house. Keely came to the door holding a hula hoop. "Phil, what's going on?" she said, surprised to see him there.

Phil sighed. "Keely, it's getting out of hand," he admitted. "I either have to marry Marla or leave town."

As upset as he was, Phil was distracted by the sound of cats meowing and circus music playing inside the house. "What was that?" he asked.

Keely rolled her eyes as she quickly shut the

door. "My mom and her friends are having a cat circus." Before he could open his mouth, she stopped him. "Don't ask."

Phil was more than willing to get back to the main problem in his life. He and Keely sat down on the back steps, and Phil said, "Marla says she loves me for what's on the inside," he complained. "Does that stink or what?"

Keely couldn't help it. She laughed.

"Keely, it's not funny," Phil said indignantly, "and it's not fair. Girls have all these rules, and we're supposed to figure out what they are."

Her eyebrows raised in astonishment. *He* was complaining that he had to figure out *girls'* rules? He should try being a girl and figuring out what *boys* were thinking. Now *that* was an impossible task. "Are you kidding?" she said out loud. "It's not easy for us, either."

"Well, I have absolutely no idea what's going on in Marla's head," he said.

"Phil, sure you do," she said gently. He looked baffled. Maybe she needed to spell it out for him. . . . "She thinks you're cute, funny, and sensitive," she explained. "The problem is she doesn't know what's going on in your head."

Phil wasn't sure where this was going, but he had a bad feeling about it. "What am I supposed to do?" he asked. "Be like Tia and kick her to the curb?"

"It's probably best just to be yourself," Keely suggested. "You're cute, funny, and sensitive. You know, *guide* her to the curb."

Phil nodded, thinking over this advice. *Guide* her to the curb.

Yeah. He could do that.

Meanwhile, Debbie Berwick was still holding that last note of "Give My Regards to Broadway" on the stage of the H.G. Wells Junior/Senior High auditorium. The orchestra was confused. The audience was baffled. Pim was delighted. This was true revenge!

And it got even better. Pim had managed to call a pizza-delivery place as she conducted the song, using quick dial on her cell phone. As Debbie was holding that note, and looking more and more desperate for air, the pizza guy came onstage with a box of juicy pepperoni pizza.

Mmm. It smells delicious, Pim thought, as she handed him the baton and reached into her pocket for money.

And still Debbie held that last note.

Then Pim pulled a nice, big cheesy slice from the box and took a nice, big cheesy bite of it.

And still Debbie held that last note.

Annoyed, Pim looked at her watch and faked a yawn.

And still Debbie held that last note! Pim couldn't believe it, but Debbie had turned her prank into a show-stopping moment.

Fine, Pim thought, irritated. She knew when she was beat. She brought the baton down to end the song. Debbie stopped singing and took a big breath of air.

And the auditorium erupted in applause and cheers.

Pim was baffled. She looked at Debbie, who was all smiles, soaking up the applause. "How could this happen?" Pim asked. "They love you."

Debbie was beaming. "Because you challenged me," she said. "You took my singing to a whole new height. Thank you!"

Debbie Berwick was thanking her for the mean trick she had played? Pim couldn't believe it. Then Debbie took her hand, inviting her to share the ovation. Together, Pim and Debbie took their bows as flowers rained onto the stage in front of them.

CHAPTER SEVEN

The next morning, Phil rushed into his English class right after the bell sounded. He was usually on time, but this morning he had to finish a special project.

Mr. Ginsberg gave him the typical glare that teachers use on any student who dares to show up late. "Glad you could join us, Mr. Diffy," he said sarcastically.

Phil ignored him and slipped into his seat in front of Marla, who leaned forward and whispered, "Where have you been, Philly Willy?"

He shuddered. Philly Willy. Well, at least he

knew that, after today, Marla would never call him that again. And it couldn't be too soon for Phil.

He turned around and said, "I was actually writing you something—a poem."

Marla's eyes widened in delight. "You wrote me a poem?"

Oh, great. She was already heading down the wrong road in her imagination, he could tell. The road that led to romance and roses and even worse things . . .

"Yeah, yeah," he said quickly, hoping to downplay what he had done. "But . . . here." He handed her a piece of paper, adding quickly. "Don't read it, though, right now."

Phil suddenly felt a cold chill. Without even turning around, he knew that Mr. Ginsberg was standing behind him and had seen the pass-off. Carefully, he turned to face the front of the room and, sure enough, he saw the teacher frowning down at him.

"Well, look who's not only late, but we're

passing notes," the teacher said, turning up the sarcasm volume at least five notches. "Perhaps you'd like to read this in front of everybody."

Why did teachers always ask that question when they caught someone passing notes? Surely by now they knew what the answer was? Phil sighed. "No, no. Thank you, though," he said. "It's not really for everybody."

And, of course, Mr. Ginsberg made the same time-honored suggestion that every teacher in the history of high school made when a student explained that a private note was not meant for public consumption.

"Oh, well, I'll read it," the teacher said. He cleared his throat and read the first few words. "'A poem by Phil Diffy to Marla Beauregard.'"

Phil could hear giggles, snickers, and even a few guffaws from his classmates. Marla looked as happy as if he had just handed her a five-carat diamond ring. This, Phil knew, was going to be bad. So, the only thing to do was get it over with. On his own.

"Okay, thank you," he interrupted Mr. Ginsberg. "Thank you. I'll do it."

Phil stood in front of the class, poem in hand, and took a deep breath. Everyone's eyes were on him. He could sense the barely suppressed laughter of the class. This is certain to be humiliating, he thought, but he had to do it. It was the only way to get Marla to understand his true feelings.

He cleared his throat and began reading the poem out loud:

"I met you in the hallway only a week ago/Your beauty so radiant, like new-fallen snow."

Marla blushed and smiled. Phil felt his heart sink to think of how he was about to crush her happiness. He went on.

"We studied our hearts out, time I'll never regret/But there's been something on my mind that's making me fret."

Marla frowned slightly. Phil stared intensely at the piece of paper he was holding. Anything to keep from watching her face during the rest of the poem!

"So here's the truth, the simplest way I know how," he said.

"We can't go on, not never and not now."

Phil sat down quickly. Marla's face looked like a storm cloud. She jumped up and marched to the front of the classroom.

As she passed him, Phil said, "Marla, I just want to let you know: it came from the heart."

Marla grabbed Mr. Ginsberg's smoothie from his desk.

"Marla, that's my coco-nana smoothie," Mr. Ginsberg protested.

She ignored him and marched back to Phil's seat, pulled his shirt collar away from his body and carefully poured the freezing smoothie—all sixteen ounces of it—down the front of his shirt.

Phil gasped in shock as the icy-cold coco-nana smoothie hit his skin. The entire class gasped in delight as they thought about what a great story they would have to tell at lunch. Mr. Ginsberg gasped in outrage and opened his mouth to say something, but Marla interrupted him.

"Save it!" she snapped. "I know where the principal's office is."

Angrily, she stalked out of the classroom, slamming the door behind her.

Phil slumped down in his seat. I don't think Marla really took that too well, he thought glumly.

Finally, English class was over. As Phil walked down the hall, a huge smoothie stain on his shirt, he saw Keely,

"Well, I did it," he told her.

"Yeah, I heard," she smiled. "It's all over campus." She laughed and shook her head. "I can't believe you broke up with her by poem."

"You told me to be cute, funny, and sensitive," Phil protested.

"But a poem?" Keely asked. Didn't he understand how a girl would feel if a boy used a romantic literary device to, well, *dump* her?

"She likes poetry," Phil said defensively.

"Not anymore," Keely shook her head. "Phil, Phil, you have so much more to learn."

Phil sighed. He knew Keely was right, he had tons to learn about girls—but first things first. "Can we start with how to get a smoothie stain out of my shirt?" he asked.

Later that day, Bradley was finally released from the custodian's closet. Wearing only an undershirt and boxer shorts, he gave his statement to a police officer, who wrote down exactly what he said.

"She only had one name," Bradley said, "Pim. Blond. Angry . . ." He hesitated, thinking back to the girl who had turned his world upside down and added in a musing voice, "yet strangely attractive."

His eyes widened as he saw the police officer take note of this.

"Hey, don't write that!" he yelled.

Sighing, the police officer erased Bradley's last remark.